Heroes & Villains

AADIYA CHAUHAN

First Published in June 2022

ISBN: 978-93-5628-214-8

BLUEROSE PUBLISHERS
www.BlueRoseONE.com
info@bluerosepublishers.com

+91 8882 898 898

Cover Design:
Geetika kandari

Typographic Design:
Namarata Saini

Distributed by: BlueRose, Amazon, Flipkart

About the Author

Aadiya Chauhan is a charming, fun-loving, 13-year-old teenage girl. When she was 3, she started learning SKATES; at 5, she started learning the art of BHARATNATTYAM (one of the supreme Indian dance form) and at 10 she started writing small stories and poems, just for fun. One of her stories got recognition at the school, which inspired her to write a book and become an author.

Aadiya is a SKETCH ARTIST and currently learning the art of pencil shading. Most of the pictures in the book are Aadiya's sketch work.

Picking Fiction & Fantasy as her genre, she started researching the subject by reading books and watching content on TV, OTT & Internet.

Aadiya hails from India, a diverse and culturally rich country, which is one of the most ancient civilization in the world. India is a country of great ancient scholars like Chanakya, Aryabhata, and the home of the first residential university of the world... 'Nalanda'. A densely populated secular country with over 400 languages, 2000 dialects, and a universe of heritage.

Aadiya belongs to an educated family, and she aspires to achieve profound knowledge to pursue her dream of becoming an author of repute.

We hope you will like her fictional work: Heroes & Villains and, also urge you to give your feedback at ascaadiya@gmail.com

Acknowledgement

I would like to take this opportunity to thank everyone who helped me start, write, and publish my book. I'd first like to thank my mother, dadi, father, and my beloved younger sister for encouraging me in my efforts to become an author. I love you all so much!!!

Special thanks to my Mom for helping me in making the sketches expressive.

I'd also like to thank the Team of BlueRose Publishers for showing faith in my abilities and making sure my book reaches your hands.

Finally, I'd like to thank you dear reader for picking up my book and if at all you liked it.   .

With warm regards

Aadiya Chauhan

About the Book

Heroes are always Heroes but is a Villain always a Villain or are the circumstances...

It isn't always kids who get into trouble and get saved by their parents, it could be vice versa...

A young optimistic girl finds this out when her famous parents are lost...

She is determined to do anything to get them back, but will it be that easy?

Find out how she does this and finds more than just her parents...

Welcome to Heroes & Villains and be part of TIARA's story...

Here's how the story goes...

After happily ever after

Have you ever wondered what a hero actually means? The main character in a film or the one who kills the villain… Right? What about a villain? That school bully, or anyone who happened to torture you? No and no.

So, once upon a time, a young princess was born. She was so fair that her name came to be Snow White. Just a sec, just a sec, pause this thing ⏸ yeah, now, you know this story, almost by heart, who doesn't? So, let me fast-forward this thing to the part I am more interested in ⏩⏩⏩. The dwarfs started chasing the evil queen. They chased and chased her until they cornered her to the edge of a cliff, but the tricky queen tried to use her stick to lift a big rock that was near her and hit the dwarfs with the rock but as you might know, whenever we use try while narrating, it often means that the incident didn't happen even though the person "tried". So, the evil queen "tried" to send the stone towards the dwarfs and there was a flash of sudden lightning exactly when she "tried" to lift the stone and that lightning fell exactly where the evil queen was standing and, no need for explanation, she fell off the cliff with the stone and two vultures that seemed to be chasing her from the beginning went behind her. Now, the dwarfs returned. They should have buried Snow White, but they didn't. They preserved her body in a glass case, instead. A few months passed and a handsome prince aka prince Florian who Snow White knew came next to the glass case. Now, don't ask me why but he kissed her, and BAM Snow White woke up. And some things happened that I am not sure of, and they all lived happily ever after.

But wait, the story didn't really end! I'd say that happily ever afters are *boring*, really, I mean if there is no problem, there's no adventure and everything is just <u>boring</u> and whoever made this world realized this and decided to have happy endings for every chapter and then start a new one. That's exactly what happened I'd say, so, Snow White and Florian got married, a whole year passed, they had a daughter and that's where I come in. Yes, I'm their daughter.

My name is Tiara. You can imagine how I look like, just imagine Snow White i.e., mom with much longer hair and blue eyes, a bit different face structure and a red dress, yes, that's me. It's said that every girl's a princess in her house then you can imagine what a real princess may be like. I literally got everything I ever wanted- loving parents and um…uh…. etc. Ok, it may not seem like this but being a princess and literally having the best parents in history just seemed enough. Although, school was boring and I didn't have a lot of friends there, I did have a friend in the castle, he is Daniel. He is super annoying but still better than having no friend at all. Just in case you were wondering, he is that hunter's son who had spared mum's life, not something that needs a reward but anyways. You know, the only thing boring about school wasn't that I didn't have lots of friends but also that there were only 3 subjects: English, science, and math. Science was fun, but math was a nightmare and English could be great if it wasn't for the "great" stories we had to learn. Let me give an example, there was a story in which an old lady was falling from a mountain and out of nowhere two birds saved her while still in the air, birds asked her that if she'd never kill a kid in her life, they will save her. They said it as if she was seriously a serial killer. She sure enough agreed and was safely put to ground; but if the story is bad, each character is weird and the old lady said to make another deal with them, she wanted to never age and to look most beautiful. I mean, seriously? Weirdest part, the birds agreed but in return trapped her somewhere underground. Ok, I can understand they might want something in return but isn't trapping someone - who can't even die thanks to the deal – underground, way too much? Anyways to get back, except for school, everything was just great, and I couldn't imagine my life without mom and dad. They just always made sure I got everything I ever wanted. I was just like both of them too, I was super kind like mom and brave like dad. Dad had taught me archery and even sword fighting and now I am much better than him. No, I'm not bragging. Maybe, I am …. a little. Anyways, everything was just great …. till it was not. When I was 10 something changed everything.

"Mom, Dad, do you have to go?" I wailed.

"Come on," mom replied. "We'd be back by 1."

 "What?" I replied a bit annoyed, "but, it's just 6 am right now."

"That means it's not long before we're back." Dad said, "and after we come back, someone's getting gifts."

"Really!" I said enthusiastically. "Then what are you waiting for? Go and come back fast!"

"Ok, then," Mom said. "Have fun."

"And," Dad said. "Don't get late for school, alright?"

"Come on, I won't," I said.

"Ok, then, bye!" Mom said.

"Bye," I replied.

I hugged them and they were off. So, they were coming by 1 am in night, I'd have to be all alone today.

Time passed till it was like 10 pm, I just passed a random thought to Daniel.

"I guess, mum and dad would be on their way by now," I said.

"Yes....um...yeah, uh, sure, they would, um...they would be back I'm sure, I'm sure they would be coming, yeah coming back" Daniel replied.

Ok, something had happened, maybe like last time they were planning a surprise of some sort and chose to tell Daniel again. Bad choice. For a moment or two, I just kept looking at him.

"What? Um...nothing's wrong......I'm just, you know I think while I speak......that makes me slow while speaking." He told. I decided to use a trick that always works on Daniel.

"It's ok, Daniel, I know, you can't trust me with a secret." I falsely wiped my tears.

"That's not true, I tell you everything. always. really."

"I know the reality, I am not a good friend, that's why it's hard to trust me." I acted as if I was crying.

"No. no. no, I do trust you. really"

"Then, tell me what you are hiding."

"Ok .... um .... Your parents are lost" "what?"

I paused, thought a bit, and said "Ya think I'm crazy, big people don't get lost"

"Funny, isn't it?"

"Daniel" I suspected he was still lying.

"What? This is the truth!" Ok, he was not.

"What do you mean they are lost? And even if they are, how do you know?"

"I'm not pretty sure but I heard Mildred and Oki talking about this and they told me not to tell you. So, yeah, this is it"

"But they were supposed to come by late at night, how did they know?"

"1 pm not a.m."

"What? Great. I mean, what the heck is going on? Why didn't those people want me to know?"

"Now, I don't know everything, ok?"

Mildred and Oki are those people who help mom and dad in making decisions regarding, well, how to rule the place. You can think of them as junior judges although mom and dad have to agree to what they suggest and maybe now that the "senior judges" were not there they made a decision themselves. A bad one. I felt mad. Now, I should know things, considering I'm the princess. So, I talked to both of them.

Anyways, I wasn't really worried about my parents actually, the whole universe recognizes them, and half the world might already be looking for them, so by the time I'd wake up, they'd be home. Now, what's the worst that can happen?

"There you are," I said. "The whole kingdom was searching for you."

"I know" Dad said. "I have something for you"

He took out a paper.

"Don't worry" Mom said. "It is a map, and it will tell you the right path when you are old enough. When you ask anything to it, it'll give you the answer."

"What do you mean?" I said confused.

"it's all on you, find us with this map" Dad said.

"What do you mean? Wait, how'd you even come here?"

I looked around and there were white clouds everywhere and suddenly mom and dad disappeared.

I woke up. It was all a dream. It was so life-like as if they came and gave me that … wait, ….in my right-hand I. had. the. MAP! Was I still dreaming? I pinched myself and it did hurt. I wasn't dreaming. Did it mean they were gone....so much so that they had to put a message in my dream? How'd they even learn that? And did it mean they were actually, actually …… gone?

"Daniel!" I screamed. "DANIEL!" He came rubbing his eyes.

"What? You really hate when I sleep, don't you?" I started crying.

"Whoa!" he said. "What happened? Why're you crying?"

In baffling words, I told him everything. Don't ask me why, but he giggled a bit and stopped himself.

"YOU'RE LAUGHING!!!" I screamed.

"Come on," he said. "I mean, Tiara, it was just a silly-billy nightmare, not urgent, and nothing to wake me up and call me here"

"There's no one else inside the castle but you in the night and this is serious, I still have the map."

"It's just a piece of paper, ok, just try asking anything to it and you'll see nothing would happen. Try it"

I didn't even answer, was he seriously serious?

"Show me where my parents are," I said to the map .

It didn't show where mum and dad were but it did show the letters "Wait till you are ready"

"See?" I said.

"Ok." He said in a little shocked way. "Maybe it is magical. but it doesn't show their location." He said still calm.

"It says I have to wait"

"How long?"

I turned to the paper.

"How long do I have to wait?"

"8 years" it said.

"What?" both of us said together.

Sketched by the Author

Now I was really mad, but I was also more worried.

"Are you sure? Is that the least limit?" Daniel asked to the paper.

"Yes, although it can be extended." The words appeared.

Daniel was always a cry baby but at this point, he kept looking at the paper in shock without even moving. I, on the other hand, took a long, harsh breath and cried. I just hugged Daniel while crying. I guess that's when he moved, he didn't say a thing but I know he was not liking the hug. He never liked hugs.

"At least, tell us where they are, I promise I won't go there," I said to the paper.

The words appeared, "You're lying" it did know everything.

"Ok, just for satisfaction, please, I swear I won't go."

"The mysterious bamboo," it said. "And also, if any of you keep a foot in the forest till 8 years pass, you won't be there to see your parents."

It sounded horrific. The night passed and none of us could sleep. We were both in two different corners of the room.

The word spread, the next morning, and almost everyone i.e., except me and Daniel went to search for them. Things got weirder when the dwarfs went to search for them and didn't return. They weren't the only ones; whoever went there either came back with nothing or didn't return, ever. Days passed like this and I was made the crown princess. It is not that different from a queen. It's just that, I can't do something politically, if it isn't agreed by the royal council and I'm not going in this boring stuff. After a certain time, we created a rule that forbids any Lavendarians from going in the mysterious bamboo. Oh wait, Lavender's where I live, so my country people are Lavendarians. So, I did wait for 8 years, 8 long years. I used to wonder why the thing had to be so strict in allowing me to go. Honestly, I wouldn't trust a piece of paper, and I didn't believe it at all but I just didn't want to take any chances.

2 days to my 18th birthday!

"I just can't wait," I said to Daniel while I was walking by the hall. "Not a lot of time left"

"Yeah," he said in a dull voice. "Great."

"You're not excited. Is it because you wanted to come too?"

"No. I'm just worried... What if you didn't return either like all of them, you know."

"Now, you're just being that annoying overprotective older brother. I'll be fine and you're saying this as if I'm supposed to go right now."

"Well, you are supposed to be at your archery practice right now. And you're also late."

"Oh yeah!"

I went for practice and came back.

The next and last thing of the day was to sit and find solutions to local problems. I sat on the throne and let the people in. Only one girl around my age came in, which means only one solution to find.

"Your majesty," she said with a bow. "It's not a big thing, just that.... well, there's this guy who sort of destroyed my dad's whole hotel"

I almost laughed and then stopped myself. The hotel only had one room so, I'm sure no one got hurt.

"It's not funny." The girls said.

"Just ask that guy to pay for it," I said

"He did pay"

"Then?"

"I can't say he is doing it purposefully, but he is like a Godzilla ruining everything in his way, and this way I think all that will be left would be the money he keeps giving after everything."

"Ok."

"Doesn't matter, and did I mention he is a prince"

"No, and how come I didn't know a prince of ...... somewhere is about to come"

"<u>My</u> point is, I think it would be insulting if some random person asks royalty to leave because, well ... he is clumsy."

"Ok, so, you want me to go and ask him to leave. Easy, I can do it."

She guided me to this prince. I was sort of surprised a prince could be this clumsy, but sure it was better than meeting the "perfect" princes that I had met earlier. She left me alone after that.

When I saw him, I realized I had seen him before, I was not surprised, I know many of the royalties. I wasn't sure of his name, though, but I think he was from South villes. He had brown hair and green eyes and he was eating an apple while leaning on a fragile fence. Remember the apple and fragile fence.

"Hey," I said. "I'm princess Tiara of Lavender. Is this a good time to talk"

"Yeah, sure." he replied. "Prince Lemon from South villes"

"You know, I found out you don't have any place to stay here."

"I don't,"

"I am very sorry that you had to go through this, and I think you should find somewhere else to stay, I mean, there aren't a lot of other hotel here, so you can maybe go to Marendelle instead, it is very similar to our place, so you'd know how our place is too, you'll like it."

"You sure about this?"

Oh no! I wish I'd thought before saying that I forgot he said he's from South villes.

"Try to go to Lorona then, it's so much cooler, yeah?"

I said tring covering myself up but I think I had done it.

"Actually, I was just gonna go to Lorona, like... first thing tomorrow morning."

I just blanked out and at the point, I just wanted to get out of there. Man, what could he be thinking of me? For a second, I just thought of an excuse to get out of there, then I finally said, "ok then, have fun, I am late for a party I must attend, it was nice to meet you. Bye."

"Bye."

Then, out of nowhere he suddenly tripped, and that too, with the fence.

Sketched by the Author

Remember the fragile fence? Now I get what the girl meant. I stared at him for a second and I although wanted to giggle, I didn't. I was actually thinking I'd look weird to him, but I think if the front person is weird, they can't find out the same about you.

He looked at the apple that fell from his hand for a split moment of second (remember the apple) and then while getting up said, "Honestly, I can't believe apples aren't banned here."

I chuckled.

"Well," I said still chuckling. "Just because one apple was poison, doesn't mean all will be."

"Woah" He chuckled. "Wish everyone thought that way"

Then I remembered my excuse and said, "Oh, the party. Bye."

"Bye."

The trees of wisdom

It was night, around 11. I got out of bed, put a hood on, and slowly went out of the castle. I was going towards the forest. The forest 'the trees of wisdom' only stayed near Lavender till 12. Wait, you seem to have no idea what I'm talking about.

Ok, so there's this forest called "Trees of wisdom" that seems like a normal forest that just often changes its location (Yes, it is normal for forests to change their own location around here); but as we all know, looks can be deceiving. So, it is a magical forest where you will find books about magic inside every tree, which is not so cool but still. The cool part is that the trees here can talk. Seven people would come in the forest each on a different day of the week or in my case, night; this group is called 'the Specials' and don't ask me why that's the name. No one created this group; I somehow knew I'm part of this since as long as I can remember and came here every Saturday. Honestly, I never met any other person from this group and I don't really care. In case, you were wondering, yes, I know magic. I most usually only came to the forest to ask for advice because as you know, there are not a lot of other people to ask for advice and there can't be another reason because I've read all the books here. According to the rules of magic, I can perform every other magic that I can imagine but there is one unique magic type that no one else can do better than me and that unique magic type is called the x. This rule applies to anyone who knows magic.

Now, I should have normally come on Saturday but I didn't. I slowly went into the forest, there was not a lot to talk about today, so I thought I'd be back quite early. I was about to say something to a tree when I heard some noise, did someone follow me? I took the arrow I had and shot it towards the voice. The arrow did nothing to the person, I had just shot it to scare and freeze the person.

"Ok," I said. "You move, and the next one's for you"

"Ok," said a familiar male voice. "won't"

Then I moved towards him to use the forgetting spell (No one is supposed to know about the group or its magic unless the other person is from the group) but then suddenly I froze where I am, in a second, I figured out, it was that guy's magic. It struck me then that maybe he was one of the Specials, after all, it was Friday not Saturday.

"Ok," I said. "I think there's some misunderstanding, I mean I thought someone followed me but"

"Wait, I know you. Tiara, right?" "………everyone knows me, I was saying" "you're one of the Specials?" He said while coming close, that's when I saw him and guess who he was. "Lemon?" I asked.

"Oh," he said. "You have a good memory."

"A: I just met you this morning so of course! And B: Get me out of this spell!"

"Oh, yeah."

Then he lifted the spell, much better.

"Ok," I said. "Well, so you're one of the Specials?"

"I thought you'd realize it earlier." He replied.

"I did, I was just checking. Anyway, you mind, if I talk to the forest today and you come tomorrow because I don't think the forest allows more than one person to be here?"

"No!"

"No?"

"Yeah, No, tomorrow I'll leave for Lorona, and it is hard to find where the forest will be at what time of the day and where exactly in which part of the city."

"Fair point, but I really have to talk to the forest, and I can't talk tomorrow because I need a nice sleep before my birthday and there's no point talking after that."

"You'll leave me in so much trouble just because you need sleep"

"When I sleep at 11, I wake up at 11. There's just a lot to do and I don't want to reduce my time."

Then a tree in front of us said "There's no rule that only one person can talk to us in a day."

"There isn't?" Lemon said.

"No," the tree replied. "Tiara can go to the north side and John can go on the south side."

"Who's John?" I asked.

"That's my real name, Lemon is just a nickname and for some reason, that's how I like people calling me."

"Ok," I replied.

I went to the north side. Then, in front of one tree, I said, "Hello"

"Tiara," said the ghostly voice of the tree. "What do you need?"

"Well," I said. "You know, I'd be going the day after tomorrow for my search, I'm just not sure about leaving the kingdom to Daniel again."

"What makes you say that?"

Sketched by the Author

"I think, he's still too irresponsible to handle Lavender, and the last time I went on that tour with Shanelle for a few days, there was a pool of ice cream in the hall and a painting was burnt in my room."

"He has grown out of it, trust me."

"That's what I'm hoping, because although I can ask Mildred to take care of the kingdom, I can't."

"But aren't they your parent's most loyal advisors?"

"Well, I was never fond of Oki or Mildred, even though they give good decisions. Upon that, it sounds weird just to say that I can leave the kingdom with Mildred or Oki and not Daniel"

"Although there is no harm in leaving the kingdom to Oki or Mildred, you should most probably take Daniel's help. Princess, try to always trust your instincts, they know the future."

"Oh, thanks ... what's the time?"

"11:15 pm"

The tree's face disappeared. I had never gone so early before but it was ok on my side. It was anyway a relief that Daniel would keep the place fine. I started to walk out when I bumped into Lemon for the third time in the day.

"Hi." I said. "again"

He laughed.

"Man" He then said. "It's been years since someone smiled back at me."

"Huh?" I said. "Why? You don't seem that bad."

"I don't know, because of my uncle maybe, ok in case you think I'm telling things you have no reason to know"

"No, no, continue, Who's your uncle."

"Clens."

"Clens? That Clens? But he doesn't look that old to be someone's uncle. How old is he? 25?"

"24. Here's the thing, you know, after he suddenly became so super famous for trying to take over Marendelle and trying to kill their queen, for some reason over the past four years, that made everyone think the whole South villes are traitors."

"I've heard of this but I'm not able to understand how your uncle is only 3-5 years older than you."

"My dad, he is the oldest of all his brothers and now that Clens is the youngest, I just happened to be born only six years after him."

"God, talk about weird family, anyways, it's ok, now you have a friend outside South villes."

"Thanks, really."

"You're welcome. Just out of curiosity, what's your X."

"I can teleport other people… but not me. It hasn't even been much use of it because we can't even tell others about the powers, and I can't teleport them if they don't want it, which is also a part of my x so yeah."

"Oh-k, still, it's much cooler than my X; wait, try teleporting me!"

"Ok, where?"

"Try, random, anywhere, you have the whole outer space… Right?"

"Ok, buckle down, then. Ready, steady, go!"

Before even I could blink, I was somewhere else. It was a beautiful green field, I looked around to see the beautiful view, when I saw a 14- to 15-year-old girl and boy staring at me. The guy looked shocked, but the girl just said, "See?" and before I knew it, I was back, I could just wonder what they were talking about.

"Man," I said. "That was wild!"

"It was, wasn't it." He replied. "So, what's your X."

"Nothing special, really. If I ever get in a situation – which I sure wouldn't – where someone tries to attack me when I have no idea, I'll dodge the attack and anyways, who's gonna come at me like that?"

"I think it's a cool one."

"I don't. Anyways, it's getting late, I've to go, bye."

"Bye."

I went back and had a really needed sleep. The next day was quick and boring. Imagine, having to decide everything for your own birthday. When I had to send invitations, I thought maybe it would be a good idea to call Lemon in the party. Although I was about to invite Renna and Chelsa too - the princess and queen respectively of Marendelle which Clens tried to take over - but they ain't the one deciding who I'll invite, right? They won't even know he is from South Villes anyway, and even if they would, I know them and I'm sure they won't judge him for something he didn't even do, I mean they're the heroes of their own story. And on the contrary, in my perspective, I think Clens just wanted to rule some place, which he couldn't as he was the youngest of all his brothers and Marendelle happened to be the first one in sight. I mean, if I'd be in his situation where I couldn't rule my own place, I'd try my luck somewhere else too, sure not the way he did but he does have some reasonable reason unlike, the one evil queen got, she is just like 'you're prettier than me! That's a crime! Don't be prettier than me! How could you do that to me!' Anyways, the day just ended like that.

Happy Birthday!!!

The next morning was just great and honestly, I was wondering what I was more excited for, finally finding my parents after a long time or the wonderful party. I mean, after waiting 8 years, the day was finally closer than ever. As I walked after getting up, everyone was wishing me happy birthday as expected, what I didn't expect was that Daniel and everyone else in the castle would give me gifts!

"What's this?" I asked. "I never planned this."

"And I thought you liked surprises," Daniel replied. "This is from my side. Surprise!"

"Aw. Thank you. Although, I thought I was anyway gonna get a lot of gifts."

"I thought you'd say that, so I even decided that half of the gifts would be donated as charity."

I chuckled. He knew me so well.

"How about all of them getting donated." I laughed.

"Sorry, the box for donation isn't that big."

"Ok, so the rest of them are yours. How about that?"

"Sorry, but everyone will get girlish gifts"

"Maybe or maybe not. Deal?"

"Deal."

We both laughed. In all those years without mum and dad, he was the only one who helped me smile.

About the party, I had invited half the world's Royals and my whole kingdom. It was about to be crowded, real crowded, and fun.

The party started with many people. I didn't expect Menzel to come but somehow, she did. shanelle, Tia, Merila, Monaya and even Laya.

"Hey," Laya asked. "You had all these decorations done? They're pretty nice."

"It wasn't me," I replied. "Daniel's been surprising me the whole day long"

"You mean that guy, I thought he is just a servant in here."

"No, not at all. You know that hunter that helped mum get away? Daniel's his son. Evil queen killed the hunter and I have no idea what happened to his mother but after that mom felt that it was her responsibility to take care of him and just took him in."

"To me, it sounds like an adopted brother's story."

"Not exactly, but yeah, can say, although I don't think anyone ever thought of him as a prince, not even he, himself."

After some time, Mel-Mel came with her mother, Marial; Lilan, and even Lemon came after that. Most of my kingdom's people came early and almost all the Royals came late. The party was going on great.

"How old did you turn today?" Asked Mel-Mel.

"Eighteen" I replied.

"Man, you are so big."

"I'd think the same if I was 8."

"You know mom and Snow White were good friends.".

"I know"

And that's why I don't talk to small kids.

"No," I said. "I never stopped learning archery or sword fighting."

"Then?" Lemon asked.

"Merila helped me learn archery and lilan helped me learn sword fighting. If you don't mind me asking, are you the king or a prince of South villes because to me I think you'd be the oldest of all your brothers, sisters, or cousins."

"I don't have brothers or sisters ...... or cousins, somehow. As for the king part, as it goes in South villes, on the eighteenth birthday, I'm either gonna take the crown or give it to someone else of my choice."

"In my case, I can take the title queen whenever I want from now on. So, you're not 18 yet?"

"My birthday is a few days later but I'm not so excited about it."

"Why? You're not sure you'd be a good king or something, because if that's the case" "Actually, I just don't wanna be a king and I don't know who to pass the throne to."

"Ok... not expected but I think that there are a lot of your uncles. Right?"

"Actually, I never wanted to be king of anywhere and I was pretty sure I'd give the crown to Clens before he made this mess, and honestly no one else knows how to rule a place. Back then, we were both best friends, but I don't know what got on him when he went to Marendelle and ......"

"You could never trust him again."

"Yeah"

I said nothing for a second and then I replied, "You know, I know Chelsa very closely and as much as I know when Renna went before Chelsa and trusted the kingdom on Clens, he handled everything well, I mean he betrayed them later but when he didn't the kingdom looked like it got the best leader, and logically speaking maybe if you give him a second chance, he might even change."

"Not sure it's the greatest idea"

"Just a suggestion."

I just kept talking to different people.

"I heard" Renna said. "That you are going in that bamboo mystery, whatever of some kind."

"Yes," I replied realizing where she was gonna lead up to.

"I just hope … um … I hope it's not the last time we meet"

"Come on, this is a birthday party and not a farewell party, you do realize that, don't you?"

"Yes, but we've been friends for a while and I just …… you get it don't you?"

"Well, I think I need to officially announce that I'm gonna be all ok, huh?"

The whole party was so fun, I didn't even realize when it was more than 12. After the party was over, I just told everyone in the castle not to wake me up, even if I sleep till 2 pm. After all, no one told to wake up as early as possible to go to the Mysterious Bamboo.

The journey has begun!

The next morning was it; I've to say as excited as I was, I was sort of nervous too, I mean this could either be a great family reunion or a terrific end. Although this thought did scare me, I didn't wait 8 years to back off at the last moment. I had announced I was to leave and there were a lot of people who came to meet me. After this, I was ready to leave.

"Well," I said to Daniel. "I'm bad at saying goodbyes. You know that."

"You know," he said. "I would have said it's still not too late to back away but all I can say is come back soon."

"Thanks, and make sure the kingdom's safe. I don't want any more ice-cream pools."

I laughed.

"You know all that was an accident...... so... bye, I think." He said.

"Bye," I replied.

I hugged him tightly.

"Okay, you didn't need to hug." He said ruining a perfectly good moment.

"Bye," I said angrily.

I did have a bag of supplies and it wasn't a long journey to the mysterious bamboo. Within an hour I was already pretty close to there. I had also packed some of the magical objects around. I didn't expect any surprises but ... if only things were that simple.

"Hey" I heard a familiar voice.

I turned around to see Lemon running, he might have come to say goodbye too.

"Hey" He repeated huffing and puffing.

"Hey" I replied.

"I figured," he said still huffing. "That I can come with you."

"Whoa, whoa, whoa, whoa, whoa, what? .... _What?_ ..._**WHAT?**_"

"I know."

"You're not coming, I'm not risking any lives, ok?"

"Hey, hey, listen. I'm an inch away from ruining my life" "By being the king, let me guess"

"Yes"

"So?"

"So, I'll be stuck within my kingdom forever and I could use some adventure before that."

"If you want to risk your life and never come back, you're welcome."

"Great then."

"I didn't mean it! No one's coming with me, and I think you have a lot of choices you're not using, anyway."

"Ok, just a reminder, just because I won't go with you does not mean that I can't go without you."

I paused, he was right, so I just gave in.

We walked and walked till we were tired. After a good amount of time, we reached the mysterious bamboo. I took out the map.

"Ok," I said to the map. "Where do we go now?"

The letters appeared: Follow the purple ribbons.

"cool" Lemon exclaimed.

Among the bamboo trees, I found one of them had a purple ribbon tied to it. After getting close to it, I saw that behind that bamboo, there was a trail of bamboos with purple ribbons tied on.

"We have to follow the trail of purple ribbons," I told Lemon.

Sketched by the Author

After walking a while, I found a big, deep-looking pit. Also, the trail of purple ribbons ended there. Did it mean they fell in the pit? Did it mean I came all the way here for nothing?

"Ok," I said to the paper, taking a deep breath. "Where do we go now?"

"Jump in the pit." It said.

I looked at the paper, for a long time and then angrily growled, "Is this thing trying to tell me that my parents are dead and if you wanna meet them again, go kill yourself. Did it mock me and gave me fake hope for 8 long years?" I screamed angrily.

I then realized that Lemon wasn't there. "Lemon," I screamed.

"I'm here." He said coming from somewhere. "I was trying to find a stone, to check the depth, you know?"

"Ok"

He then threw the stone down inside the pit. I have to say the stone traveled a long distance, but if we track the sound, I think, it was like an underground tunnel or a slide. I looked at the map, "Is it safe to go inside this thing?" I asked.

"Safe enough." The words appeared. I think I learned to trust this thing after all .

"Ok," Lemon said. "This sounds cool. I'll go first."

He went in. I was still hesitant but I didn't come this far to turn back. I stepped in; it rather felt like a slide for a very long time before I slipped. And suddenly, everything went black.

under the ground

I opened my eyes. I seemed to be inside a dark cave-like thing. I couldn't remember where exactly the tunnel's exit was, I looked around to see that I was in a much bigger cave, and the part where I was, was somehow locked by magic. I was basically in a cell. I couldn't see anyone else, not even Lemon. I could hardly see anything. When my eyes adjusted to the dark, I tried to find the exit just so I know where to go when I find everyone. I looked here and there and then I saw a small hole outside the cell I was in.

"HEY!" I screamed. "Anyone here?"

That's when it hit me, someone had put me in there! I could have just fallen where I was, but it could only be if the hole was somewhere on my head, but it didn't seem the same now. I tried to see how many other cells I could see but it was hard to see anything besides nothing. Great, I had trapped myself and now I was gonna starve to death.

"HEY!" I screamed again. "Some voice, please."

"So" I heard a female voice. "The little princess is finally awake."

"Alright. Who are you and why have you trapped me here?" I paused and then said. "And have you been keeping my parents here?"

"Oh, so you don't know me."

"Oh, no, I don't, who are you?"

"I'd say the villain of your mother's story."

"What?" I paused and took a long while. "You are ... the evil queen!"

"Quick one."

"Are you a ghost? Or am I actually dead and even if, how come I am in hell 'cause there is just no way for you to be in heaven and this place does look like hell."

"You talk a lot and everything you say sounds boring, just like your annoying mother."

I didn't know what to say on this.

"Where's mum and dad?" I screamed. "And lemon? Where are they?"

"Oh," She replied. "You wanted them alive? Sorry, they're done for."

Everything paused for a moment. After waiting so long to come so far, this is what I get. I somewhere could not believe that this was happening.

"They're not here?" I said softly.

I went and sit back.

"What about the dwarfs?" I said in a slow and low voice.

"Oh," she said. "They didn't seem to have a good reason to live either."

I was quiet. All those memories, all that time, all that wait for nothing. I even made a kingdom lose its future king. If only I would've moved on.

"I don't believe you," I said softly in an unsure way.

"Oh, you don't need to believe," she said. "The truth won't change with that."

I was quiet and I didn't say anything. The whole day passed. I didn't cry. I didn't even move. I was just shocked. So much, so that I could stay where I was forever. I worried about everything, even the fact that Daniel might not be able to do anything alone. Why didn't I risk coming here ages ago?

Some truths be untold

I was still in shock when the evil queen, wait no, Regina (Her real name as she is not the queen anymore) rudely passed me some food.

"Sure," I said. "Everyone falls for the poison trick."

"Oh, if I had to kill you, that would have been easy, but I want to see you suffering."

I was being a lot stressed at the moment and now I think the angry side of me just screamed, "You crazy woman, what have I ever done to you? What did my family ever do to you? How can you be so crazy, just a psychopath, you did all this just because mom happened to be prettier than you?"

"Oh, life is unfair, isn't it? Full of hate for no reason, huh?"

"You'd have to be so self-conscious to do that."

"If I weren't like this, I might not have got it all"

"Come out of the illusion, you're living in a cave, no worse, under the ground, you didn't get a thing. That paper led me here, it will get me out."

Sketched by the Author

"Oh, and I thought you were smart. I was the one who crafted that dream. This is my map, and it won't help you if I don't want it to, and who do you think got the purple ribbons there? Magic can do anything, especially dark magic."

"I'll find another way out, I, I can do anything."

"Then do that anything."

I stood there while she went. I tried to think of every smallest detail possible about a plan, even about Regina, there would be some clue that would get me out. I kept thinking. In doing so, I randomly remembered that boring legend. Then I suddenly remembered how everyone thought Regina died. Wait, the vultures chased Regina, right? Just like in the legend where the two birds chase, An Old Woman! Can that mean that Regina was the old lady in the legend, now that she was disguised? That would explain why she is here and alive! The English lessons, finally put to use. Putting it together, Regina fell off the cliff, was saved by the vultures made a deal with them, ended up in this place in the process, kidnapped my parents, sent me a dream, and locked me here. But wait, I'm missing something, why did she call me after 8 years, she didn't need to do that.

Anyway, if this is true, she can't kill any kid that would include anyone under 18. That meant that she couldn't have possibly killed Lemon because he said his 18th birthday was coming later. She lied! She lied just to make me feel miserable and hopeless. This could mean that maybe, just maybe she didn't kill my parents either, and anyway if she wanted to make me suffer, she would without a doubt want the same for mum and dad. Suddenly, I came back to the optimistic and hopeful me.

Now I had to find a way to get to Lemon, he might be able to transport me somewhere. I looked here and there, but nothing in sight. Then I looked at the things that I packed. I had a few Reality Charm arrows. They are amazing things and they almost look like they're made of smoke; if we shoot it towards a place, we can create illusions, sort of change the reality. If we shoot it towards a person, we can paralyze them into saying the truth, to show reality but it all lasts for half an hour only. I looked in my bag and there was a shovel lying in the corner. I had a brilliant idea, lucky me!

I took the Reality Charm arrow and shot it in the middle of the cell, now when Regina would look here, she'd feel that I am right there when I'm not. It could help in doing everything in shadows. Now, any person who knows magic can tell that the prison she made can't be broken from the front side, but I realized she missed thinking about the other sides! I had realized that earlier but I didn't wanted to make an escape plan at that point.

I could easily shovel to reach Lemon. I got to work, I shoveled, and made a tunnel to a different cell.

There was no one there. I kept shoveling my way to different cells until I found someone in a cell. That was Happy, one of the dwarfs.

"Happy," I said in excitement.

"Who are you?" He replied.

"You don't look at all happy, I am Tiara, remember?"

"Yes, yes, I did feel you familiar, what are you doing here?"

"Sure, you did, well, long story short I got stuck here while looking for mum and dad and I think I know a way out."

"You do?"

"Yeah, but no time to talk. I have to shovel to find a cell in which there's this guy who can help us out."

"Leave it to me! I am just an expert now that I'm a dwarf."

"Great then."

He took the shovel and did everything pretty fast. I think at this speed we may reach pretty fast. I went into the tunnel while he dug. We went into few other cells and found a woman sitting in one of them.

"Hey," I said to her. "I am Tiara and I think I can say I'm here to save you"

"Liar!" She screamed, which is something not expected. "Nothing's gonna happen, I've been stuck here" "You wanna get out or not because I'm okay with leaving you here." I was too stressed already to keep up with this. She just followed us on this one. We started digging again and found an empty cell.

"Nothing's happening," she screamed. "I never should have listened to you."

This girl was acting as if she needed a reason to scream.

I wanted to say - If you want, you're free to go away - but I didn't.

While we dug more tunnels, she just kept saying things and I just had to put up with it. Even Happy was tired now.

The girl decided to help and took the shovel, something better.

The Plan

Finally, we dug into another cell and found Lemon in like 1000 years.

"Tiara" he said.

I hugged him.

"Man," I said. "You don't know how long we've been looking for you."

"Now" The woman screamed. "How do I get out? I knew you've been tricking me! Nothing's gonna happen."

I turned to Lemon, "Do me a favor, get her out on the surface. Seriously."

"As you wish, princess," he said laughing. And whoosh! The girl disappeared. Some relief. I could be stuck here 900000 years and still not act like that woman did.

"You sent her outside, right?" I asked.

"Yeah. So, you look like you have a plan." He said.

"Oh, yes, I do."

I told him what I had planned. It would take a while so I used another reality charm arrow here, Regina would never know what is really going on.

Now, he had to transport me to any cell with a prisoner inside. Then, he has to transport me and the other person in his cell, then he could transport that person out. And then, this way when everyone would be out, we both could think about how to get him out too.

So, the plan was in action. He kept teleporting me here and there and we got a lot of people out in a few moments. I even got to see some other dwarfs like Bashful, Grumpy, and Doc. After a while, I was in a cell and I saw DAD!

"Dad" I screamed.

"Tiara," he said weakly. "Is that really you?"

"Yes, yes, yes. Are you okay?"

"What are you doing here?"

"Just doing some hero stuff and saving you."

"It is dangerous here."

"Too bad, you didn't teach me to be scared, and anyways I know just how to get you out, you just need to want to get out of this cell."

"Okay."

Just then we got transported into Lemon's cell.

"Prince Charming!" Lemon screamed. "Oh, I've been your biggest fan since my childhood."

"Lemon," I said not interested at all. "Not the time."

"What are you doing exactly?" Dad asked.

"That's a long story," I said. "Just believe me and you'll be out of this place and just wait for me for a moment."

"Ok," he said.

Whoosh. He was gone too. I slowly got all the dwarfs and even mom. I knew they were all alive! Slowly and gradually almost everyone was done. Then, when he once tried to get me in another cell with a prisoner under there, it didn't work. This showed everyone was done, yes!

"Now," I said. "How do we get you out?"

"Let's think." He replied.

"Regina might already have discovered that I'm not in that cell, we've to think fast!"

We were the only two over there and the arrow we were using would erase the illusion any moment.

"Maybe," he said. "We could dig our way up."

"Yes," I said excitedly. "Of course, we can. Can't believe I didn't think of that! You're digging. I'm too tired."

"Yeah. Okay. I mean, how hard can it be?"

Now, he started digging with the shovel, and gradually, we were almost out. Right now, I became sure the journey had ended, so much so that the only thing I was thinking was how dirty my dress would be. Then, when he made the final move. A sudden, bright light blocked my vision.

Someone pulls back

As I tried to open my eyes, I suddenly felt pulled back, hard and before I knew it, I was pulled back to where I was, and I could guess Regina used magic (You can recognize people's magic just like you can recognize their voice) when I was a step away from getting out. Great! She had also filled up the tunnel I was trying to use to get out, with magic. She is seriously skilled with magic to do all this so quickly.

"Alright," I said "I, anyway, needed someone to try my sword's skills with. Pretty sure, you can't defeat me."

"Oh," She replied. "Really, let's see."

I don't know her any great but I hoped she would take up such a challenge. I think, this way I could easily climb up if I manage to trick her, to the hole on the other side (The one outside the prison walls). And yes, she was dumb enough to take her sword out.

"Alright," I said.

I was too good at sword fighting to even worry. I was easily able to dodge her attacks but she wasn't bad either.

Sketched by the Author

I realized that this way it would be hard to get out, I mean, I won't wanna kill her or something and even if I would have, she can't die, remember?

I was hoping that by this time Lemon would somehow teleport me back but no sign of that either. I don't know what he was doing.

I was on the verge of winning, when Regina's magic made the Reality Charm arrow stuck at the cell come towards me. This was supposed to be the end. The arrow traveled at a great speed. It came closer and closer while I had no idea. It would paralyze me when it hits, and Regina could use that time to kill me!

Sketched by the Author

It was one millimeter away from me, less than a second before I could die but suddenly, I automatically fell as if something was pulling me under, and at the last second, I dodged the arrow without even knowing that. Before, I could realize anything, the arrow went towards Regina and she got paralyzed by it. That's when I realized what she was doing. What a backstabber! I was also shocked actually but I felt happy. Remember that my x is to dodge any attack when I have no idea something or someone is attacking me. That's why I fell to the ground instead of getting hit. Now, that she was basically given truth serum I could ask her anything.

"Well," I said to the paralyzed Regina. "Turns out I win! Ok …… um just out of some childhood curiosity, did you actually do so much just because some stupid mirror told you that my mom was prettier than you."

"No." She replied.

"Knew it … wait, what? What did you say?"

"I didn't do it just because I wanted to be fairest of all."

I was shocked. I never imagined this. I think that half an hour is a pretty long time, so I can afford to listen to what actually happened.

"Then?" I asked. "Why then would you become my mom's sworn enemy?"

"She ruined my life." She replied.

"How?" I asked.

"I was always encouraged to be fair, to be pretty, if I want power. I was a good person before I married Snow White's dad. He was never a good king, he killed thousands. Somehow, he was a good dad. He gave Snow everything she wanted. I was only there because Snow White needed a mother. He treated me like nanny for Snow White. He humiliated me, always. I kept quiet, I didn't want to lose the position of honor, that I somehow received. I finally decided to speak up, once and that is when I accidentally pushed him out of a window. I was given the power but the whole world believed that I murdered him. I decided if the world couldn't believe that I was a good person, I'd rather be the bad person."

"What was mom's fault in this?"

"Snow White was the one who spread this rumor that I murdered the king. She might not even remember this today, how she misunderstood me and made me what I am now. Then I treated her the way he used to treat me. At this time, I got obsessed with beauty and whenever I saw Snow's face, I felt she didn't deserve the beauty she got. I still didn't feel to do her any harm. When I got the magic mirror, I realized I was fairest of all and that again made me feel more powerful, while listening to the mirror, I felt that it understood me and knew who I actually was, until the mirror said snow is prettier than me; I suddenly felt that she gained a higher position than me; all the rage of all those years came together and made me do what I did."

"But didn't you at all regret this after coming here?"

"I did, but slowly I started blaming her for this too."

I paused.

"Ok, but," I said. "Why didn't you bring me here, when I was 10 considering you didn't wanna kill me?"

"Because even though I act the toughest, I couldn't bear to see a child lose her childhood, considering my own childhood was miserable."

I was silent. I wanted to leave her and go now but, there was this annoying voice I'd call my instincts that said that I couldn't leave her like that. I suddenly got reminded of what the tree in the trees of wisdom said: try to always trust your instincts, they know the future. This started hovering in my mind. I looked at the hole leading out and suddenly I had an idea!

"Ok," I said. "Please, please, please tell me you never break a deal."

"I don't." She replied.

"I was counting on that."

I got out of the hole at the point, I can't explain how good I felt on being out and seeing the light again. Lemon would be some distance away as he used a different hole, remember? I think I would just go to the trees of wisdom. Then, I suddenly saw Lemon very close actually. I didn't want to explain this to him but then I thought maybe he could teleport me to the trees of wisdom.

"Lemon," I screamed.

"Hey!" He replied. "You, okay?"

"I would be more than okay if you'd just teleport me back,"

"Well, when I got out, I felt you were behind me. I hurriedly used the forgetting spell. It was only after that I realized you weren't there; your parents were there and as you know we can use the forgetting spell only once in a day so I couldn't possibly teleport you in front of them. It was only now; I figured an excuse to get here."

"I'll forgive you if you teleport me to the trees of wisdom."

"Why do you have to go there?"

I told him everything and unexpectedly he said that he'd love to help Regina. Turns out I'm not the only weird person around.

"Come on," he said. "1, 2, 3, go!"

And BAM! I was in the trees of wisdom.

"Hey," I said to one of the trees in front of me.

"Hi, Tiara," said the tree's ghostly voice. "What do you want?"

"I want to reverse the curse given to Regina, how do I do it?"

I was expecting the tree to warn me not to do it, but the tree just replied, "Cross 12 more trees right from here, ask the vultures."

"Wait a sec" I said. "You mean the vultures are one, I mean, two of the specials."

"Yes"

Wow, two days ago I knew no other Specials, and today I know three of them. Cool!

I went where the tree told me to go and there they were.

"Hi," I said.

"Who are you?" one of them asked.

"I'm Tiara," I replied. "I was hoping you'd tell me how to reverse Regina's curse so that she'd get out of the underground."

"Do you know what you're doing?" the other one asked.

"I think so," I replied.

"Sorry we aren't gonna help ya." they both said together.

"Why not?" I asked.

"She deserved where she went." The first one said.

I paused but then I said, "Everyone thinks that. But I think when we think someone is bad, we don't realize that no one's born bad, and that something very sad happened to turn them like this. 8 years ago, I didn't trust my instincts and let my parents go, I don't wanna make the same mistake of not trusting my instincts again."

Well after my great speech, they only looked at me strangely and then started whispering things to each other, then they stopped.

"I'll tell you." The first one said. "But whatever she does is on you."

"Don't say we didn't warn ya!" the second one said.

"Well," I replied. "I somehow know I won't regret it."

"She has to sign here." Both of them said together showing a document. Man, they'd have to have it for a long time. I read it. It only asked her to leave the gift of beauty she got from the deal and accept her true self. To me it didn't look like a big thing, but I sure think Regina won't like it. That's exactly when I came back to the mysterious bamboo.

"So?" Lemon asked.

"They want her to sign this," I replied.

He read it.

"I think," he said. "She might not exactly agree easily."

"I wish she'd agree without a fight," I told him. "I'm too tired. Anyway, just teleport me."

He did. I was back in that dark, dingy place.

"Regina," I said. "I'm just here to talk."

"You're back," Regina's voice said that seemed to come out of nowhere. "A bad choice."

"I'm here to free you from this prison if you want."

She didn't say anything for a moment.

"And why would you do that?" She asked.

"I don't know," I replied. "Sometimes, you just listen to your instincts, I guess."

She suddenly didn't look in a mood to attack anymore.

"How do I know," she asked. "That this isn't a trick?"

"You don't," I said. "You just have to trust me. Like how I'm gonna trust you not to cause trouble when you come."

She kept silent. then, she said "deal."

I could tell even in the dark that she was smiling.

Although, I wasn't sure if she'd like to leave her beauty behind, she wanted to leave this place more than anything. She signed the paper and she looked way different now. She didn't look bad, but I think age did affect her. She tried getting out by the hole and it worked. We were right in front of Lemon and my parents were somehow there too.

"Mom, Dad," I said and hugged them tightly. Mom and dad looked so happy. That's when Regina stepped out, and you can imagine their natural reaction. I explained to them what happened. When none of them still looked convinced, I said "Maybe talking to her would sound like a better option."

I got out of there as they talked. I think they might actually understand this way.

I stepped out and Lemon left them too. I felt a kind of satisfaction as I leaned on a bamboo tree. After all the years, I got them out and even got a grandma i.e., if she'd like me to call her that and if this all "talking thing" worked.

"Thank you," I said to Lemon. "I couldn't have done this without you."

"You're welcome," he said with a smile.

Then, I slowly went and kissed him. We both smiled.

That's when I heard sounds of laughter coming our way. It was mom, dad, and Regina or should I say, grandma. They seemed to get along easily this time.

A happy ending

So, when I came back, Daniel surprisingly hugged me and actually cried, none of which I thought would happen.

"Man," I said. "And I thought you weren't a hugger."

After that life became easy. Lemon passed the throne to Clens; I know not expected; Regina tried to become a better person; As per me, I was the happiest person on the planet; again!

Turns out a villain is only a person who's already too tortured. Maybe that school bully is only troubling you because they're being bullied by someone else themselves, you never know. I have heard a hero helps those most in need (which, on this part should be a villain); but on my part, I'm still not sure what a hero means but what I'm sure a hero does not mean is torturing villains who're just already tortured people; and if it does, I'm no hero.